KT-375-081

PUFFIN BOOKS

The Return of the
Killer Cat

Anne Fine lives in County Durham. She has written numerous highly acclaimed and prize-winning books for children and adults.

The Tulip Touch won the Whitbread Children's Book of the Year Award, *Goggle-Eyes* won the Guardian Children's Fiction Award and the Carnegie Medal, *Flour Babies* won the Carnegie Medal and the Whitbread Children's Book of the Year Award and *Bill's New Frock* won a Smarties Prize.

Tuffy's misdemeanours in *The Diary of a Killer Cat*, *The Return of the Killer Cat*, *The Killer Cat Strikes Back* and *The Killer Cat's Birthday Bash* have delighted mischievous children all over the world.

Anne Fine was named Children's Laureate in 2001 and was awarded an OBE in 2003.

annefine.co.uk

Books by Anne Fine

The Diary of a Killer Cat
The Return of the Killer Cat
The Killer Cat Strikes Back
The Killer Cat's Birthday Bash

Jennifer's Diary
Loudmouth Louis
Notso Hotso
Only a Show
The Same Old Story Every Year
Stranger Danger?
The Worst Child I Ever Had

For older readers
A Pack of Liars
Crummy Mummy and Me
Flour Babies
Goggle-Eyes
Madame Doubtfire
Step by Wicked Step
The Tulip Touch

ANNE FINE

The Return of the
Killer Cat

Illustrated by Steve Cox

PUFFIN

PUFFIN BOOKS

Published by the Penguin Group
Penguin Books Ltd, 80 Strand, London WC2R 0RL, England
Penguin Group (USA) Inc., 375 Hudson Street, New York, New York 10014, USA
Penguin Group (Canada), 90 Eglinton Avenue East, Suite 700, Toronto, Ontario, Canada M4P 2Y3
(a division of Pearson Penguin Canada Inc.)
Penguin Ireland, 25 St Stephen's Green, Dublin 2, Ireland (a division of Penguin Books Ltd)
Penguin Group (Australia), 250 Camberwell Road, Camberwell, Victoria 3124, Australia
(a division of Pearson Australia Group Pty Ltd)
Penguin Books India Pvt Ltd, 11 Community Centre, Panchsheel Park, New Delhi – 110 017, India
Penguin Group (NZ), 67 Apollo Drive, Rosedale, North Shore 0632, New Zealand
(a division of Pearson New Zealand Ltd)
Penguin Books (South Africa) (Pty) Ltd, 24 Sturdee Avenue, Rosebank, Johannesburg 2196, South Africa

Penguin Books Ltd, Registered Offices: 80 Strand, London WC2R 0RL, England

puffinbooks.com

First published 2003
This edition published 2010 for The Book People Ltd,
Hall Wood Avenue, Haydock, St Helens, WA11 9UL
1

Text copyright © Anne Fine, 2003
Illustrations copyright © Steve Cox, 2003
All rights reserved

The moral right of the author and illustrator has been asserted

Set in Baskerville

Made and printed in England by Clays Ltd, St Ives plc

Except in the United States of America, this book is sold subject to the condition
that it shall not, by way of trade or otherwise, be lent, re-sold, hired out, or otherwise
circulated without the publisher's prior consent in any form of binding or cover other
than that in which it is published and without a similar condition including this
condition being imposed on the subsequent purchaser

British Library Cataloguing in Publication Data
A CIP catalogue record for this book is available from the British Library

ISBN: 978-0-141-33722-7

www.greenpenguin.co.uk

Mixed Sources
Product group from well-managed
forests and other controlled sources
www.fsc.org Cert no. SA-COC-1592
© 1996 Forest Stewardship Council

Penguin Books is committed to a sustainable future
for our business, our readers and our planet.
The book in your hands is made from paper
certified by the Forest Stewardship Council.

Contents

1: *How it began*

OKAY, OKAY! SO slap my teensy little furry paws. I messed up.

Big time!

And okay! Tug my tail! It all turned into a bit of a one-cat crime wave.

So what are you going to do? Confiscate my food bowl and tell me I'm a very bad pussy?

But we cats aren't *supposed* to hang about like dogs, doing exactly as we're told, and staring devotedly into your eyes while we wonder if there is some slipper we can fetch you.

We run our own lives, we cats do. I

like running mine. And if there's one
thing I can't stand, it's wasting the
days and nights when the family are
on holiday.

'Oh, Tuffy!' fretted Ellie, giving me
the Big Farewell Squeeze. (I gave her
the cool blink that means: 'Careful,
Ell! Stay on the right side of cuddle

2

here, or you'll get the Big Scratch in return.') 'Oh, Tuffy! We'll be away for a whole week!'

A whole week? Magic words! A whole week of sunning myself in the flower beds without Ellie's mother shrieking, 'Tuffy! Get out of there! You're flattening whole patches!'

A whole week of lolling about on top of the telly without Ellie's father's endless nagging: 'Tuffy! Shift your tail! It's dangling over the goalmouth!'

And, best of all, a whole week of not being scooped up and shoved in next-door's old straw baby basket and stroked and petted by Ellie and her soppy friend Melanie.

'Ooh, you are lucky, Ellie! I wish *I* had a a pet like Tuffy. He's so soft and furry.'

Of course I'm soft and furry. I'm a *cat*.

And I am clever, too. Clever enough to realize it wasn't Mrs Tanner coming to house-and-cat-sit as usual . . .

'. . . no, she suddenly had to rush off to her daughter in Dorset . . . so if you hear of anyone who could do it

4

. . . only six days . . . well, if you're *sure*, Vicar. Yes, well. So long as you're comfortable with cats . . .'

Who cares if the vicar's comfortable?
I'm the cat.

2: *Home not-so-sweet home*

UH-UH! MR Houseproud!

'Off those cushions, Tuffy. I don't think you're supposed to be lolling about on the sofa.'

Excuse me! Had the vicar not noticed it was me he was talking to? So what was I supposed to be doing? Mopping the floor? Tapping away on the computer? Digging the garden?

'Tuffy! Don't scratch the furniture.'

Hell-oooo? Whose house? His? Or mine? If I want to scratch furniture, I'll scratch it.

Worst of all: 'No, Tuffy! I'm not

opening a fresh tin until you've
finished this.'

I took a peek at 'this'. It was hard.
It was lumpy. It was yesterday's grub.

And I wasn't eating it.

I walked away. The last thing I
heard was Reverend Barnham calling
after me: 'Come back and finish your
supper.'

In his dreams! I was off out. I met
up with the gang – Tiger and Bella

and Pusskins – and told them I hadn't had supper. They were hungry too, so we sat on the wall and had a bit of a yowl about where to eat.

'Fancy peeling the pepperoni off a leftover pizza?'

'Fish without chips?'

'I could murder a nice bit of steak.'

'Who's thinking stir-fried beef strips with scraped-off soy?'

In the end we went Chinese. (Love those ducks' feet!) Tiger strolled off on a smell tour down the alley to find the right place, and then we played 'Rip the Bags'. (We all won that one.) Before you knew it, it was a pleasant supper on the wall.

'Very tasty.'

'Excellent.'

'Nice choice. We must remember to eat here more often.'

'And generous portions. Here is a family not afraid to waste food properly.'

Unlike my friend, the vicar. Next morning he was still shoving the dried-up grub in front of me. 'Tuffy,

10

I'm not opening a fresh tin. If you were truly hungry, you'd eat this.'

Oh, would I? I didn't think so.

While he was waiting, the vicar stared out of the window. 'Look at that mess in the garden! Greasy paper wrappings! Ripped-up takeaway food cartons! And that awful yowling kept me awake for hours. Don't think I'm letting you out again tonight.'

I might be deaf to nagging, but I
have ears. Thanks for the warning,
Reverend! I crept upstairs and patted
at the latch on the small bathroom
window until it was the way I like it:
far enough down to look as if it was

still closed from yesterday; far enough up for one good paw push to open it.

As for that mess in the garden – don't knock it! It was breakfast.

3: Mistake!

OKAY, OKAY! So it was a bit mean to hold that night's Talent Contest right under the vicar's bedroom window. Bella sang 'Beooooooooooooooooooo-ootiful Dreeeeeamer'. Tiger sang 'Rolling Along to New Orleeeeeeeee-eeeans'. Pusskins did his 'Yodelling Song', and I did my brilliant imitation of Ellie when the car door slammed on her finger.

Still, no need for the vicar to get his knickers in such a twist. 'If I catch a single one of you, I'll have your guts for garters!'

I didn't come home early. But
everyone needs their sleep, so in the
end the gang and I split up, and I
strolled back. It was a beautiful
morning. The only thing spoiling it
was his voice. I could hear him three
streets away.

'Tuff-eee! *Tuff*-eeee!'

I crept along in the shadow of
next-door's hedge. Melanie was
leaning over it. 'Please, Reverend
Barnham,' she interrupted him. 'Does
praying *work*?'

He stared at her as if she'd asked
him something like, 'Do trains eat
custard?'

Melanie tried again. 'You're always saying to people, "Let us pray". Well, does it work?'

'Work?'

'Yes. Do people get what they pray for? If I prayed really, really, really hard for something, would I get it?'

'What sort of thing?' Reverend Barnham asked her suspiciously.

Melanie clasped her hands together. 'A pet all of my own to cuddle. A pet who is soft and furry and warm, just like Tuffy behind the hedge here.'

Well, thank you, Melanie! I took off, fast. And he was chasing me. That's why, instead of going up the apple tree as usual, I took that flying leap on to the handle of the lawn mower, and then up in the pear tree.

But when you get to the top of

that, you find you have only two choices . . .

1. You can jump from the top branch through a closed and locked bathroom window. (Uh-uh! My best escape route rumbled!)

2. Or you can go back down, then jump from the lowest branch back

on the mower handle, and down on
the grass again.

Which – since my flying leap
upwards had sent the mower spinning
– turned out to be impossible as well.

4: Stuck up the tree

GIVE HIM HIS due, he tried
everything. He cooed. He cajoled.
He wheedled. (There's not much
difference between cajoling and
wheedling, except wheedling's more
whiny.)

Then he tried threatening. 'You'll
miss your supper, Tuffy.' (Scarcely a
threat to make me tremble, given
what was on offer.)

Then simple nastiness. 'You can
stay up that tree till you rot, Tuffy!'
(Charming.)

The fact is, I wasn't faking it. I

was dead stuck. Don't think I would
have *chosen* to spend half of my
morning on one side of the tree,
listening to him getting rattier and
rattier . . .

'Come down at once, Tuffy! Get
down here!'

. . . and the other half on the other
side, listening to Melanie on her

knees, with her hands together and
eyes closed, praying and praying . . .

'Oh, please, please send me
something soft and furry, just like
Tuffy next door, to put in my straw
basket and cuddle. I'll give it my
comfiest pillow to sleep on, and feed
it fresh tuna and cream.'

Fresh tuna! Cream! Didn't the little

lady know I had missed my breakfast?

After a while, I couldn't stand listening any longer. I moved back to the other side of the tree. (Who could blame me?)

The vicar was clearly getting hungry too. After a while, he left off threatening me and went inside to make his breakfast. (No yesterday's grub for him, I noticed. Through the window came the sweet smell of sausages and bacon.)

They always say that breakfast is good for the brain. It certainly stoked up his little patch of grey matter because, a few minutes later, he came down the garden carrying a stool.

And climbed on it.

And he still couldn't reach me.

I wasn't being difficult. I really wanted to come down. If he had

managed to reach up even nearly
high enough, I would have been
prepared to drop in his arms. (I might
have scratched him a little, but hey!
Cats are famous for being ungrateful,
so why worry?)

In fact, I actually tried to help,
creeping towards him along the
branch. But then the branch started

sinking. (That's diets for you. Hard to keep to.) And as the branch got thinner towards the end, I weighed it down more and more, till it practically turned into a dry ski slope.

I didn't dare go further, so I stopped.

But watching the branch sink under

my weight did seem to have given the
vicar an idea . . .

5: Genius!

HE WENT IN the garage, fetched out a
length of tow rope and came back
under my tree. Climbing on the stool,
he tossed one end of the rope over
my branch.

'Right!' he said grimly. 'Slip knot!'

I yowled. Was he planning to *hang*
me? I don't often wish I could talk, but
I admit that at that moment I wished I
could rush back to the other side and
drop a suggestion to Melanie: 'Hey,
Sugar! Give over praying for something
soft and cuddly, and phone the cops.
This vicar is trying to kill me.'

29

He muttered his way through the slip knot. 'Round and through, then round and through again.'

(I kept up the yowling.)

He tugged the knot tight, then pulled on the rope. I dug in with my claws. The branch came down, but not quite far enough for him to reach me.

He tried again. This time, he managed to pull the branch a little further down. (I nearly fell.) But it still wasn't quite far enough.

'Jump!' he said. 'Jump the last bit, Tuffy!'

I gave him the blink.

'Jump, Tuffy!' he said again.

I glowered at him. (If you had taken a rolling pin to my eyes, and flattened them, they couldn't have got any slittier. The look I gave him could

have crawled through a closed
venetian blind.)

'Chicken!' he said.

Okay, okay! So I spat at him. What
are you going to do? Throw your
woolly at me? He called me a
chicken! He was practically begging

for it. He as good as said, 'Spit in my eye, Tuff!'

So I did.

He glowered back at me.

And then – oh, creepy, creepy! The glower turned into a little smile.

'Ah-ha!' he said.

I'll tell you something. People who don't really like you shouldn't say 'Ah-ha!' It makes those who know they aren't liked very nervous.

Especially if they're stuck up trees.

'Ah-ha!' he said again, and hurried back to the garage.

The next thing I knew, he was backing the car out. For one horrid fur-shivering moment I thought he was planning on knocking my tree down. But then he stopped, put on the brake and got out again.

He stood at the back end of the car and knotted the other end of the rope round the bumper.

'Right!' he said, admiring his handiwork. 'I think that's so strong it'll pull the branch down low enough.'

I stopped my pitiful yowling. I

suddenly had hopes of getting down before I died of old age in that tree.

If I am honest, I thought he'd hit upon a brilliant idea to rescue me.

I thought the man was a *genius*. I was *impressed*.

6: *More fool me*

WELL, MORE FOOL me. Don't get me wrong. The plan went well at first. Tickety-boo. He got back in the car, switched on the engine and drove away from the tree at almost no miles a hour –

   – carefully –

   – carefully –

until the rope went taut. The branch went down as planned –

   – lower –

   – lower –

until my way back to the ground was practically a gentle downward stroll.

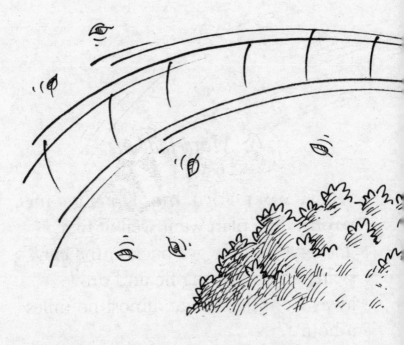

'Brilliant!' I told myself. 'I can manage that. Leftover sausage and bacon rinds, here I come!'

And I picked my way down the branch –

– tippety –

– tippety –

– and that's when his foot slipped

on the pedal.

The car shot forward. The rope
snapped under the strain. The forked
tree branch became a giant leafy
catapult –

– and I became a flying cat.

Wheeeeeeee! Watch me go! I flew
in one beautiful rainbow-shaped arc

right over the tree top. (I tell you, I wouldn't want to do it again, but the view from up there was spectacular. Spectacular! You could see as far as the gasworks.)

But, after that, of course, the only way was
d
  o
    w
      n.

7: *Splat!!!*

SPLAT!!!

Straight into Melanie's little straw basket.

Okay, okay! No need to sob in your pillow! I may have splatted some of the not-so-cuddly little creepy-crawly things that were scurrying about on the cushion. I didn't actually end up picking any tiny crushed corpses out of my fur; but still, it would amaze me if all those ants who saw me coming got away in time.

Hearing the *thwack!* of my landing, Melanie broke off her prayer. She

opened her eyes, and, seeing me in her straw basket, looked up to heaven.

'Oh, thank you! Thank you!' cried Little Miss Stupid and Soppy. 'Thank you for sending me exactly what I asked for – something all soft and furry to cuddle, just like Tuffy.'

Just *like* Tuffy?

Did she think I was sent from heaven? How soft *is* this girl?

But hey! Let's not be nasty about Melanie. I could have fetched up in a lot worse places than a cosy soft cushion in a little straw basket.

She carried me inside and kept her promise. Cream! Tuna! (Were you expecting me to slide off home to nose through some three-day-old pellets of catfood?)

Then she sat down and stroked my

43

fur while she chose a name for me.

'Pussywussykins?'

Sure, Melanie. If you want me throwing up on your pillow each time you say it.

'Little Baby Munchywunchykins?'

Just try it, and I'll scratch you.
Hard.

'I know. I'll call you Janet!'

Janet? What planet is she from? For
one thing, I'm a boy. And, for
another, have I – have you – has
anyone, anywhere – *ever* heard of a
pet cat called Janet?

But the cream was fresh. The tuna
was delicious.

So Janet was staying. Oh, yes. Janet
was warm, well fed and comfortable.
Janet was staying.

8: Sweet little pussy

GO ON, THEN. Snigger. So I looked a
bit of a pussy cat, wearing that lacy
bonnet. And the doll's frilly nightie
was too big for me. What are you
going to do? Ban me from Fashion
Week?

I had a good time, being Janet.
The meals came three times a day.
(Three times a day! That nightie was
headed for being a perfect fit, any
time next week.) I had steak bits, and
haddock, lean chicken, sausage ends.
You think of what you really love to
eat most, and then imagine soppy

little fingers feeding you, mouthful by mouthful, and you'll see why I stayed.

The only problem was the endless yelling from next door.

'Tuffee! Tufff-*eeee*! Where ARE you?'

Melanie settled me back down comfortably in the straw basket, and

stood on tiptoe to peep over the
hedge.

'The vicar's still looking,' she told me
sadly. 'Poor Tuffy! He's still missing. I
hope, wherever he is, he's warm and
dry and comfy and well fed.'

I purred.

She turned back. 'Oh, Janet! I'm so glad to have you.'

She squeezed me so tight, I gave a little warning yowl. Not a smart noise to make, just over the hedge from someone looking for a cat.

His head appeared. 'You've found him!'

I stayed well down in the basket.

Melanie's kind, but she's not bright. 'Who?'

'Tuffy!'

'No. That was my own cat yowling. That was Janet.'

'*Janet?*'

'She was a gift.'

I'm glad that Melanie didn't say 'A gift from heaven'. That would have made him even more suspicious. As it was, he narrowed his eyes at me.

Disguise! I thought, and simpered
in my basket.

The bonnet and nightie obviously
confused him a little, but he did have
a go. 'His face looks very like Tuffy's.'

I purred in a friendly fashion.

'But Tuffy never made a noise like
that.'

(No. Not in *your* presence, Buster!)

The vicar's eyes gleamed. 'Melanie,'
he said. 'Do you mind if I do one
tiny little test to assure myself it's
not Tuffy?'

He came through the gate, and
picked me up.

Talk about tests! Some have to walk
through fire. Others are sent on seven-
year-long voyages. Some have to go
and make fortunes. Others kill
dragons, or set off to find the Holy
Grail.

Nobody's *ever* had a test like this.
He scooped me out of the basket.
He held me up.
He looked me in the eyes. (I didn't blink.)

He said, 'Nice pussy! Pretty, pretty, pussy!'

He said, 'Sweet, sweet pussy!'

He said, 'Who's a clever little girl pussy, then?'

And all I did was purr.

He put me back in the basket.

'You're right,' he said to Melanie. 'It isn't Tuffy. And I can't think why I

ever thought it was in the first place.'

Phew!

More cream. More tuna. Here we come!

9: Rumbled

GO ON. Admit it. You wouldn't have gone home either. You would have stayed the whole week, just like I did, stuffing your face and getting fatter and fatter.

By Saturday night, I was as big as a barrel. There were splits down the sides of my seams. I was bulging out of the nightie.

And that's when the gang came looking for me.

They peeped in the basket.

'Tuffy? Tuffy, is that you?'

I was a bit embarrassed. I disguised
my voice.

'No,' I explained. 'I'm Janet. Tuffy's
cousin.'

Bella stared at the fur bulges
bursting through the nightie.

'So what happened to Tuff? Did
you *eat* him?'

I gave her the blink. 'No.'

'So where is he?'

I shrugged. Maybe it was the most energetic thing I'd done in nearly a week. Anyhow, the seam of the nightie split, and a whole lot more of my bulges fell out at the sides.

'Doing a striptease, are you?' Pusskins said, then added rudely, 'Fatso!'

That set them all off.

'Furball!'

'Tub o' lard!'

I narrowed my eyes. I made the tiniest little noise. The *tiniest*. Everyone said afterwards that I was the one who started it. But I wasn't. It was hardly a hiss at all. It was more like a *purr* really.

I blame Bella. She should never have put out her paw and patted me. 'Come on, guys! Until Tuffy turns up, let's have fun with this great furry beachball!'

So I thwacked her.

So she thwacked me back.

And that's how the fight started. It was quite a big flurry, with flying fur and shreds of nightie floating all over. At one point, the bonnet ribbons nearly strangled me, but I wriggled

60

free, and took all three of them on again.

But suddenly, with my disguise in tatters round the lawn, everyone cottoned on.

'Hey, guys! It *is* Tuffy after all! It's Tuffy!'

'Yo, Tuff! At last!'

'Found you!'

And that's the moment Melanie came down the garden, carrying my third meal of the day.

The others stepped back respectfully.

'Fresh cream!' sighed Bella.

'Real tuna!' Tiger whispered.

'Lots!' said Pusskins.

But Melanie didn't put it down as usual.

'Tuffy,' she said to me sternly.

'What have you done with Janet?'

I tried to look all Janety. But, without the lace bonnet and nightie, it didn't work.

Melanie looked around. And, I admit, if you were expecting to find

your precious new pet, it did look a
bit bad. Shreds of fur and nightie and
bonnet all over.

'Oh, Tuffy! Tuffy!' she wailed. 'You
bad, bad cat! You've torn Janet to
pieces and eaten her! You *monster*!'

The others turned and fled and left me to it.

'You monster, Tuffy! Monster! *Monster!*'

10: How it ended

SO THAT SORT of explains what all the fuss was about when the car drew up at the roadside, and out spilled the family.

'Tuff-eee!' yelled Ellie, catching sight of me through Melanie's open garden gate. She rushed in to greet me. 'Tuff-eee!'

Then she spotted Melanie, sobbing her eyes out.

'What's the matter?'

'Your cat ought to go to prison!' Melanie shrieked at her. 'Your cat's not a cat. Your cat's a *pig*. And a *beast*.

And a *murderer*!'

I went back to trying to look all sweet and Janety.

Ellie's eyes had gone huge. She looked at me sternly and her eyes filled with tears. 'Oh, Tuffy!' she whispered, horrified. 'What have you *done*?'

I like that. Very nice! Aren't families supposed to stick up for one another? Charming of Ellie to believe the worst, just because her best friend is watering the lawn with her tears, and there are bits of shredded nightie all over.

I was pretty put out, I can tell you. I stuck my tail up in the air and started the huffy strut out of there.

Wrong way! Straight into the vicar's arms.

'Gotcha!' he said, scooping me up

68

before I'd even spotted him lurking
behind the pear tree. 'Gotcha!'

And that's how, when Ellie's mother
finally strolled through the gate, she
found the vicar holding me the way

that a cat lover doesn't hold a cat.

And staring at me the way a cat
lover doesn't stare.

And saying things I don't believe a
vicar ought to say.

Ever.

He won't be asked to cat-sit in our house again.

Anyone sorry?

No. I didn't think so.

Byeeee!

Puffin by Post

The Return of the Killer Cat – Anne Fine

If you have enjoyed this book and want to read more,
then check out these other great Puffin titles.
You can order any of the following books direct with Puffin by Post:

The Diary of a Killer Cat • Anne Fine • 9780140369311	£4.99
'A brilliant tale of catastrophe and pussy pandemonium' – *Daily Telegraph*	
The Killer Cat Strikes Back • Anne Fine • 9780141320984	£4.99
'This is enough to make a dog laugh' – *Carousel*	
The Killer Cat's Birthday Bash • Anne Fine • 9780141324364	£4.99
The fourth hilarious title in the bestselling Killer Cat series.	
Notso Hotso • Anne Fine • 9780141312507	£4.99
'A wickedly funny tale' – *Carousel*	
Roll Over Roly • Anne Fine • 9780141303185	£4.99
'Can Anne Fine do no wrong?' – *Books for Keeps*	

Just contact:

Puffin Books, C/o Bookpost, PO Box 29,
Douglas, Isle of Man, IM99 1BQ
Credit cards accepted. For further details:
Telephone: 01624 677237
Fax: 01624 670923

You can email your orders to: bookshop@enterprise.net
Or order online at: www.bookpost.co.uk

Free delivery in the UK.
Overseas customers must add £2 per book.

Prices and availability are subject to change.

Visit puffin.co.uk to find out about the latest titles, read extracts and
exclusive author interviews, and enter exciting competitions.
You can also browse thousands of Puffin books online.